W9-BAR-917

Hoppy Birthday, Jo-Jo!

Pippa Goodhart ★ Georgie Birkett

Green Bananas

Crabtree Publishing Company
www.crabtreebooks.com

PMB 16A, 350 Fifth Avenue,
Suite 3308,
New York, NY 10118

616 Welland Avenue,
St. Catharines, Ontario
Canada, L2M 5V6

Goodhart, Pippa.
  Hoppy birthday, Jo-Jo! / Pippa Goodhart ; illustrated by Georgie Birkett.
    p. cm. -- (Green bananas)
  Summary: Jo-Jo wishes she were small like her new baby sister Roo until
Dad says Jo-Jo is big enough to have a birthday party with invited guests,
jumping games, and hidden presents.
  ISBN-13: 978-0-7787-1025-7 (rlb) -- ISBN-10: 0-7787-1025-4 (rlb)
  ISBN-13: 978-0-7787-1041-7 (pbk) -- ISBN-10: 0-7787-1041-6 (pbk)
  [1. Babies--Fiction. 2. Growth--Fiction. 3. Birthdays--Fiction. 4.
Parties--Fiction. 5. Kangaroos--Fiction.] I. Birkett, Georgie, ill. II.
Title. III. Series.
  PZ7.G6125Ho 2005
  [E]--dc22   2005001574 LC

Published by Crabtree Publishing in 2005
First published in 2004 by Egmont Books Ltd.
Text copyright © Pippa Goodhart 2004
Illustrations copyright © Georgie Birkett 2004
The Author and Illustrator have asserted their moral rights.
Paperback ISBN 0-7787-1041-6
Reinforced Hardcover Binding ISBN 0-7787-1025-4

Pick a
Pocket

Hide-and-Seek
Cake

Hoppy
Birthday
Party

For the Australian Jo I know and love,
Josephine Clarke
P.G.

To Hannah and Kevan's new baby
(The Little Moose)
G.B.

Pick a Pocket

A new baby came to Jo-Jo's house.

"Jo-Jo, meet Baby Roo," said Mom.

"That's MY pocket!" said Jo-Jo.

"You're too big for a pocket now,"

said Mom.

7

Baby Roo went in Jo-Jo's old crib.

"That's MY crib!" said Jo-Jo.

"You're too big for a crib," said Dad.

"No I'm not!" said Jo-Jo.

"Come and have a big girl hug,"

said Mom.

"No hug!" said Jo-Jo.

"Do you want to help me plan your birthday party, Jo-Jo?" said Mom.

"No, no, no!" said Jo-Jo.

Mom and Dad went looking

for Jo-Jo.

She wasn't in the kitchen.

She wasn't in the garden.

She wasn't in her bedroom.

"Where are you, Jo-Jo?" they called.

At dinner Jo-Jo asked, "Where is
Baby Roo?"

"Asleep. She is too little for buns."

"Oh," said Jo-Jo.

"Baby Roo is too little for lots of things," said Mom. "But you are big enough to have friends for a party."

"Can it be a hide-and-seek party?"

said Jo-Jo.

Hooray!

"It can," said Mom.

"Baby Roo can come to it too,"

said Jo-Jo.

Hide-and-Seek Cake

"It's my party today!" said Jo-Jo.

"Goo goo," said Baby Roo.

"Let's make a cake," said Mom.

They went to the store. They got

eggs and flour and sugar.

They got a big bag of candy.

"Are they for my cake?" asked Jo-Jo.

"Yes," said Mom.

Yummy!

Mom didn't cook the cake in a

cake pan. She cooked it in a bowl.

Mom dug a hole in the cake.

Jo-Jo put icing and candles on the cake.

"No candy on top," said Mom.

Jo-Jo's party was in the backyard.

"Where is everybody?" said Jo-Jo.

Jo-Jo found Ted.

She found Ziggy.

She found Poppy.

They all found Wantab.

"Time for cake," said Mom. "Cut

the hide-and-seek cake, Jo-Jo."

Hoppy birthday,
dear Jo-Jo ...

31

Jo-Jo cut the cake. Lots of candies were hiding inside!

"Hoppy birthday to you, Jo-Jo!"

Hoppy Birthday Party

Jo-Jo and Poppy and Ted and Ziggy
and Wantab played party games.

Hopscotch. Potato sack races.

And jumping for apples.

They played pick-a-pocket.

"Time for presents," said Dad.

"I can't see any presents," said Jo-Jo.

"You have to find them!" said Dad.

Jo-Jo looked to the left.

She looked to the right.

"Look up," said Mom.

Jo-Jo picked a banana, and

opened it.

"Look down," said Dad.

"The red flower!" said Jo-Jo.

It's a teddy bear!

"Our present is too big to be wrapped," said Dad. "So I will wrap you up instead, Jo-Jo!"

Dad led Jo-Jo into the house.

"Now look!" said Dad.

"A new room! All for me! And with a
bunk bed!" said Jo-Jo. "Oh, thank you!"

They all played jumping to catch the
stars until it was time to go home.

47

"I like being a big girl," said Jo-Jo.

"And I do like Baby Roo."

"Good," said Mom.

"Goo," said Baby Roo.